For Emaline and Quinn. -J. E.

For Willow—Mommy & Daddy love you even more
than Elwood loves birdies! -N. W.

STERLING CHILDREN'S BOOKS
New York

An Imprint of Sterling Publishing
1166 Avenue of the Americas
New York, NY 10036

STERLING CHILDREN'S BOOKS and the distinctive Sterling Children's Books logo
are trademarks of Sterling Publishing Co., Inc.

Text © 2015 by Jill Esbaum
Illustrations © 2015 by Nate Wragg
Art direction and design by Merideth Harte

ISBN 978-1-4549-0879-1

Distributed in Canada by Sterling Publishing
c/o Canadian Manda Group, 664 Annette Street
Toronto, Ontario, Canada M6S 2C8
Distributed in the United Kingdom by GMC Distribution Services
Castle Place, 166 High Street, Lewes, East Sussex, England BN7 1XU
Distributed in Australia by Capricorn Link (Australia) Pty. Ltd.
P.O. Box 704, Windsor, NSW 2756, Australia

For information about custom editions, special sales, and premium
and corporate purchases, please contact Sterling Special Sales at
800-805-5489 or specialsales@sterlingpublishing.com.

Manufactured in China
Lot #:
2 4 6 8 10 9 7 5 3 1
06/15

www.sterlingpublishing.com/kids

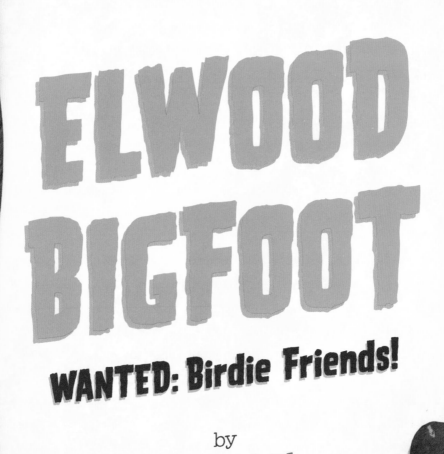

ELWOOD BIGFOOT

WANTED: Birdie Friends!

by
JILL ESBAUM

illustrated by
NATE WRAGG

STERLING CHILDREN'S BOOKS
New York

Every morning, Elwood Bigfoot sipped sassafras tea and watched the sunrise.

Alone.

Every afternoon, he roamed the forest, digging roots and picking berries.

Alone.

Every evening, he waited for dark, then
crawled into his bunk to sigh at the ceiling.
 Alone.
 Elwood couldn't have stood so much
aloneness, if not for . . .

Birdies!

Elwood loved birdies. Each flash of feather,
each chirp and cheerful song helped him feel less
alone. Whenever a birdie swooped by, Elwood
hollered, "COME BACK, BIRDIE! BE MY FRIEND!"
But no birdie ever came back.

One spring day
he was gathering
mushrooms when,
far above, a nuthatch
knocked loose a
small twig . . .

PLICK!

And Elwood was struck with an idea so brilliant he danced for joy.

"I'll live in a tree! *Then* birdies will like me!"

Nobody had ever hauled and hammered so eagerly.

Elwood's new home had everything his old one didn't: woodsy smells, breezy pockets of sunshine, and, best of all, birdie neighbors.

He couldn't wait to make friends. But how?
The birdies seemed awfully shy.

Hmm. Maybe if he looked and acted more
birdie-like. . . .

He rushed uphill and down,
gathering feathers.

He whittled a handsome beak.

He even made birdie feet to
strap atop his own.

"Perfect," he said. "I'll fit right in."

Elwood climbed up, up, up
and gingerly settled onto a
branch. There!
  Already, he felt more
birdie-like.

When a chickadee gobbled a caterpillar, so did Elwood.

When a sapsucker drummed a tree—*rat-a-tat-a-tat*—so did Elwood.

When an indigo bunting landed nearby, Elwood sang, "Choo choo, sweet-sweet-sweet."

And the bunting answered! "Chew, chew, sweet-sweet-sweet!"

Elwood shouted for joy.

Oh, no! The birdies flew away!
Elwood flew after them.

Elwood blinked back tears. The ground was hard.
So was making friends.

But by morning, he had another idea.

"I'll have a party!" he said. "Everybody loves a party."

So he delivered a few invitations, made a few appetizers, hung a few decorations.

"WELCOME, FRIENDS!" he bellowed. "C'MON OVER!"

Nobody did.

And he tried *everything*.

"HERE, HAVE A PARTY HAT!"

"CARE FOR A SHAGBARK SWIRL?"

"SHAKE A LEG! DO THE BOOLA-BOOLA!"

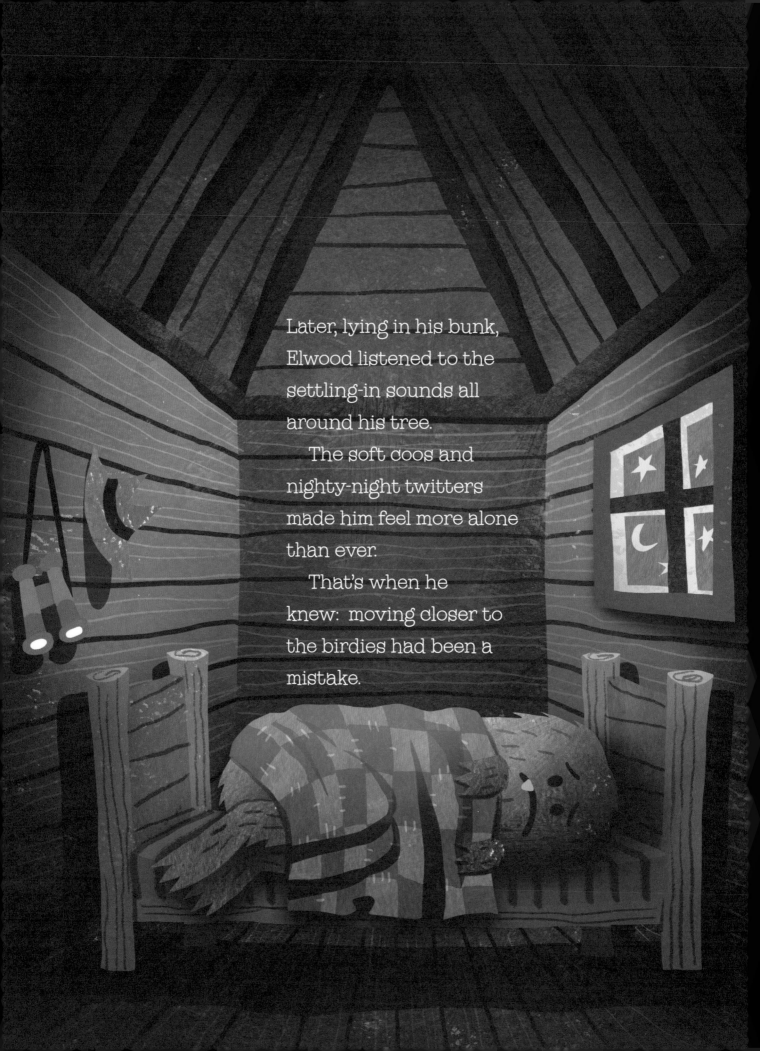

Later, lying in his bunk, Elwood listened to the settling-in sounds all around his tree.

The soft coos and nighty-night twitters made him feel more alone than ever.

That's when he knew: moving closer to the birdies had been a mistake.

Elwood was half asleep when a joyful "Twee-twee-TWEET!" made him smile. He saw a little birdie bouncing on a twig, trying to squeeze in a few more minutes of fun before bedtime.

"Birdies sure do like to have fun . . ." he mumbled.

Then he sat up. "Hey, wait a minute. Birdies like to have fun!"

Elwood was sure this was his best idea yet.
It was also a lot of hard work.

But what were a few sore muscles
(and stubbed toes and pounded thumbs)
after so many years of alone?

Still the birdies kept their distance.

Elwood began to sweat. BIRDIELAND *had* to make the birdies like him. It just *had* to.

He gobbled beetles from *The Sassafras Snack Shack.*

Belly-flopped into *Songbird Springs.*

WATCH! YOU SIT HERE, YOU FLIP THIS LEVER, THEN *KA-BOOM!* YOU FLY-Y-Y-Y!

Demonstrated the *Chick-a-BOOMerang* again and again . . .

Elwood lay there, bruised and heartbroken.

But then he felt something land on his ... well, never mind.
It was light and ticklish as it hopped up his back and
down one arm. Elwood looked down and was surprised
to see—a birdie!

Ever so s-l-o-w-l-y, he opened his hand to reveal a few
beetles still stuck there.

Elwood was too pooped to dance and holler.
He could only smile. Other birdies swooped in,
and something occurred to him:

Did a dancing, hollering bigfoot *scare* little
birdies? Elwood barely. Even. Breathed.

After awhile, though, he did manage to pinch himself. *Ouch!*
Nope, this wasn't a dream. Elwood was awake. And he had
friends. Birdie friends. Finally!

Summer was magical.
Singing up the sun.

Sharing sweet berries.

Slumber parties under the stars.

Once the birdies got to know him, Elwood could even cut loose . . .

. . . without ruffling any feathers.

By autumn, Elwood had forgotten what alone felt like.

And while some of his new friends had to fly south . . .

Take care, Tallulah!
Ādios, Diego!
See you in the spring!

. . . most stayed. Because no place else on earth had what Elwood's place had.

The snacks? The wave pool? The rides? Nope.

It had Elwood.